JR. GRAPHIC AMERICAN LEGENDS

JIM BOW[redacted]

Andrea P. Smith

PowerKiDS press
New York

Published in 2012 by The Rosen Publishing Group, Inc.
29 East 21st Street, New York, NY 10010

First Edition

Editor: Joanne Randolph
Book Design: Planman Technologies
Illustrations: Planman Technologies

Library of Congress Cataloging-in-Publication Data

Smith, Andrea P.
Jim Bowie / by Andrea P. Smith. — 1st ed.
    p. cm. — (Jr. graphic American legends)
Includes index.
ISBN 978-1-4488-5196-6 (library binding) — ISBN 978-1-4488-5230-7 (pbk.) —
ISBN 978-1-4488-5231-4 (6-pack)
1. Bowie, James, d. 1836—Juvenile literature. 2. Pioneers—Texas—Biography—
Juvenile literature. 3. Alamo (San Antonio, Tex.)—Siege, 1836—Juvenile
literature. 4. Texas—History—To 1846—Juvenile literature. 5. Frontier and
pioneer life—Texas—Juvenile literature. 6. Bowie, James, d. 1836—Comic
books, strips, etc. 7. Pioneers—Texas—Biography—Comic books, strips,
etc. 8. Alamo (San Antonio, Tex.)—Siege, 1836—Comic books, strips, etc. 9.
Texas—History—To 1846—Comic books, strips, etc. 10. Frontier and pioneer
life—Texas—Comic books, strips, etc. I. Title.
F389.B8S64 2012
976.4'03092—dc22
[B]
                                                          2011001720

Library of Congress Cataloging-in-Publication Data

Manufactured in the United States of America
CPSIA Compliance Information: Batch #PLS1102PK: For Further Information contact Rosen Publishing, New York,
New York at 1-800-237-9932

Contents

Main Characters

James (Jim) Bowie (1796–1836) **Legendary** soldier and fighter in the Texas army. He is known for his famous knife, which became known as the Bowie knife.

Rezin Pleasant Bowie (c. 1700s –c. 1800s) Jim Bowie's brother. He was known as one of the "wild Bowie brothers."

William B. Travis (1809–1836) Scout in the Texas army. He commanded the forces in the Battle of the Alamo.

Antonio López de Santa Anna (1794–1876) Army general and president of Mexico. He led the **attack** on the Alamo and had all of the Texas defenders killed.

Stephen Austin (1793–1836) The Father of Texas. He helped colonize Texas by bringing families from the United States into the region, which was part of Mexico at the time.

JIM BOWIE

AS THEY GOT OLDER, THE BOWIE BROTHERS WERE STILL WILD. THEY STRUCK A DEAL WITH THE PIRATE JEAN LAFITTE.

AFTER THE BOWIE BROTHERS BOUGHT THE SLAVES, THE BROTHERS **SMUGGLED** THEM INTO THE COUNTRY.

THEN THEY COLLECTED THE **REWARD** FOR TURNING THEM IN.

THE DUEL TURNED INTO A FIGHT, AND BOTH SIDES FIRED GUNS AT EACH OTHER.

AFTER FIRING HIS GUN, JIM PULLED OUT A LARGE KNIFE AND KEPT FIGHTING.

PUT DOWN YOUR SWORD.

NO!

JIM AND HIS FRIENDS WON THE FIGHT. AS WORD SPREAD, HE BECAME A LEGEND, AND SO DID HIS "BOWIE" KNIFE.

A FEW YEARS LATER, JIM LEARNED ABOUT THE LOST MINES OF SAN SABA. HE SAID GOOD-BYE TO HIS WIFE, URSULA, AND WENT LOOKING FOR THEM.

THEY SAY THERE'S SILVER LEFT IN THE MINES.

WE'LL BE RICH!

YOU THINK THE INDIANS WILL LET US PASS THROUGH HERE?

THAT'S WHAT THEY TOLD ME.

I WAS WRONG!

WE'RE UNDER ATTACK!

THE ATTACK TURNED INTO A MIGHTY BATTLE.

LOOK BEHIND US!

THEY'RE TRYING TO BURN US OUT!

JIM'S SMALL BAND OF MEN HELD OFF OVER A HUNDRED INDIANS. EVEN THOUGH JIM NEVER SAW THE LOST SILVER MINES OF SAN SABA, HIS REPUTATION AS A FIGHTER GREW.

THE MEXICAN FORCES MARCHED ON JIM'S CAMP.

LUCKILY JIM WAS PREPARED TO MEET THE MEXICAN FORCES.

THEY CAN'T SEE US IN THIS FOG.

WE CAN USE THE FOG TO SURPRISE THEM.

AFTER THREE TRIES, JIM AND HIS MEN WERE ABLE TO DEFEAT THE MEXICAN FORCES.

THE TEXAS ARMY HELD OFF SANTA ANNA'S FORCES FOR THIRTEEN DAYS.

SANTA ANNA'S FORCES WERE TOO STRONG, THOUGH. THEY BROKE THROUGH AND STORMED THE ALAMO.

JIM BOWIE DIED THAT DAY, ALONG WITH THE REST OF THE TEXAS DEFENDERS.

Timeline

Spring 1796   Jim Bowie is born in Kentucky.

1803   Bowie's father, Reason, movies his family to Louisiana.

1819   Bowie and his brothers buy enslaved Africans from Jean Lafitte and smuggle them into the United States.

September 19, 1827   Bowie takes part in the Sandbar Fight.

1830   Bowie moves to Texas from Louisiana.

April 25, 1831   Bowie marries Maria Ursula de Veramendi.

November 21, 1831   Bowie, his brother, Rezin, and some other men successfully battle 164 Native Americans near the San Saba River.

1833   Antonio López de Santa Anna declares himself a dictator of Mexico.

October 28, 1835   Bowie's men defeat 300 Mexican soldiers near Mission Concepción.

January 18, 1836   Bowie arrives in San Antonio.

February 23, 1836   Santa Anna's troops march into San Antonio. The Texans flee to the Alamo.

February 24, 1836   Bowie falls ill.

March 6, 1836   Santa Anna storms the Alamo and kills all the defenders, including Bowie.

April 21, 1836   Texas becomes independent from Mexico.

Glossary

attack (uh-TAK) An act of trying to hurt someone or something.

claim (KLAYM) Document saying that something belongs to you.

defeat (dih-FEET) To win against someone in a game or battle.

duel (DOO-el) A formal combat with weapons fought between two people in front of witnesses.

insulted (IN-sult-ed) Treated rudely or shamed.

legendary (LEH-jen-der-ee) Having to do with a person who has been famous and honored for a very long time.

reputation (reh-pyoo-TAY-shun) The ideas people have about another person, an animal, or an object.

responsibility (rih-spon-sih-BIH-lih-tee) Something that a person must take care of or complete.

reward (rih-WORD) A thing, usually money, given to someone who has done a good job.

scoundrel (SKOWN-drel) Someone who does not treat others fairly, breaks the law, or does bad things.

scouting party (SKOWT-ing PAR-tee) A group of people who are sent ahead to explore an area and then report back to a group leader.

slaves (SLAYVZ) People who are "owned" by another person and forced to work for him or her.

smuggled (SMUH-guld) Sneaked something banned into the country.

volunteers (vah-lun-TEERZ) People who offer to work for no money.

Index

Web Sites

Due to the changing nature of Internet links, Power Kids Press has developed an online list of Web sites related to the subject of this book. This site is updated regularly. Please use this link to access the list:

www.powerkidslinks.com/JGAM/bowie